Amos's
Killer Concert
Caper

Gary Paulsen

═══════

Amos's Killer Concert Caper

CULPEPPER ADVENTURES

A YEARLING BOOK

Published by
Dell Publishing
a division of
Bantam Doubleday Dell Publishing Group, Inc.
1540 Broadway
New York, New York 10036

ISBN: 0-440-40989-6

Printed in the United States of America

January 1995

10 9 8 7 6 5 4 3 2 1

OPM

Amos's
Killer Concert
Caper

Chapter · 1

Duncan—Dunc—Culpepper was in his driveway washing his dad's car. His best friend for life, Amos Binder, was helping him. Actually, Amos was holding the water hose over the top of the car while Dunc did all the work. Amos had more important things on his mind. He was rereading an article from the entertainment section of last week's newspaper.

"The rock band Road Kill will be appearing two nights only, at the civic center." Amos forgot about the hose in his hand and pulled the article closer. "This is perfect."

"Hey, watch what you're doing. You're drowning me." Dunc grabbed the hose. "Who cares about a sick rock band with a gross name like that, anyway?"

"Melissa," Amos said dreamily.

When it came to Melissa Hansen, Amos lost all sense of reason. He was head over heels in love with her, and if Melissa liked something, Amos made a valiant effort to like it too. Except in the case of her favorite food, liver and onions. He just couldn't quite bring himself to put liver to his lips, no matter how hard he tried. He finally gave up and figured that he would fake it until after they were married.

Dunc turned off the water. "Those guys in Road Kill are warped. They dress like they raided a Dumpster, and they can't even write a real song. Their last hit repeated the same line over and over all the way through the whole song. I don't know about you, but I get a little tired of hearing 'Whatcha gonna do about it' after about the twenty-fifth time."

"Correction." Amos lowered the paper.

"They only repeat that line twenty-three times, and then they say 'uh-huh' twice, right before they end the song."

"Whatever." Dunc touched up a spot on the windshield. "I don't know what Melissa sees in those guys. The lead singer, Raunchy Roy, looks like a porcupine with his hair sticking up like that."

"Melissa thinks the band is misunderstood. She thinks their songs have a deeper meaning than just the words."

Dunc stared at him. "Melissa told you that?"

"Not exactly. I heard it from Tracy Stevens, who heard it from Lori Johnson, who heard it from—"

"Amos. How do you know it came from Melissa?"

"Simple. Heather Thomas heard it from Rachel Lackey, and she heard it straight from Buffy VanGilder." Amos folded his arms, satisfied.

Dunc scratched his head. "I know I'll probably regret asking, but what does all this have to do with Melissa?"

Amos rolled his eyes in unbelief. "Everybody knows that Buffy VanGilder is Melissa's third-best friend."

"So?"

"So if Buffy likes the band, then it follows that Melissa probably does too."

"Amos, sometimes your logic astounds me."

"Me too. Now what are we going to do about my problem?"

"What problem?"

"Gee, Dunc, for a smart guy, you're sure making me explain a lot of stuff to you today."

"So humor me."

"It's like this. Road Kill is going to be in town for two shows. If Melissa really likes these guys and if I can get tickets, well—the rest will be history."

"So what's the problem?"

"I called the ticket office. Tickets are going fast. They'll probably be sold out soon."

Dunc frowned. "I still don't get it. If you want tickets, why don't you go buy some?"

"That's just it. I can't. You see, I loaned all my money to my sister."

"Since when do you loan money to Amy? I thought you said she never pays you back."

"She doesn't. But there was this little matter of the flood in my mom's bedroom."

"What did you do this time?"

"It was mostly Amy's fault. She was ironing her cheerleading uniform in my mom's room when I heard the phone ring. I figured it was Melissa calling to see if I knew about the concert. I was in a hurry, because you know how she likes me to get it on that all-important first ring?"

Dunc nodded. He had given up arguing with Amos about Melissa. It was hopeless. Amos was convinced that the law of averages was in his favor. Melissa couldn't go on ignoring him forever.

"You should have seen me, Dunc. I was really moving. I made it to my mom's bedroom door by the middle of that first ring, jumped for the center of the bed, and flattened out to reach the phone with my right

5

hand. My fingertips were touching it. I almost did it this time."

"Almost?"

"Just as I started my jump, my toe caught the electric iron cord and jerked it out of the plug. The whole iron landed on the bed with me. You know, they really don't make those rubber waterbed mattresses like they used to. That iron melted a hole in it so quick, I nearly drowned."

"Did you answer the phone?"

Amos shook his head. "Amy got to it first. She said it was an encyclopedia salesman and hung up. I think she's just jealous."

"So you had to pay off Amy to keep her quiet?"

Amos nodded. "Yeah, we agreed to blame the whole thing on Scruff. She says the money's just a loan. Of course she lies."

Dunc rubbed his chin. "Let me see if I understand your problem correctly. You've got to have two tickets to a concert that takes place this weekend, they're selling out fast, you don't have any money or any possible hope of getting any, and you want me to help."

Amos nodded again. "That about covers it. Got any ideas?"

Chapter·2

"This isn't exactly what I had in mind. I was hoping you were going to be a little more creative." Amos stepped off his bike and pushed it down the sidewalk behind the civic center.

"You said you needed money." Dunc pushed his bike behind Amos. "When I heard that Mr. Whitman, the manager of the civic center, had broken his leg and could use some help to get the place ready for the upcoming concert, I called and offered our services."

"I know. But I wasn't thinking about getting a job where you had to do work and stuff. Do you realize how big this place is?"

"What did you have in mind? Robbing a bank?"

"No, better. I thought maybe we could stand on the sidewalk by a busy intersection with a sign that said 'Donate to a Worthy Cause' or something like that."

Dunc stopped in front of a little white house in back of the civic center where Mr. Whitman lived. "Somehow I don't think getting you and Melissa tickets to a weirdo rock concert would qualify as a worthy cause."

"You're really too hard on these guys. Sure they have a disgusting name, they paint their faces green and black, and their songs are awful, but other than that, they're okay."

Dunc raised his hand to knock on the door. A little man with bushy white hair and a cast on his right leg pulled it open. "What can I do for you, sonny?"

"Hi, Mr. Whitman. It's Dunc. Dunc Culpepper. I'm the one who called you about the job cleaning the civic center."

The old man scratched his head. "Job?"

"You said we could sweep the center to get it ready for this weekend's concert."

"I did?"

Amos pulled on Dunc's sleeve. "He obviously doesn't remember. Come on, it's not too late to make it to the intersection and hold up that sign."

Dunc shook Amos's hand off. "Don't you remember, Mr. Whitman? The Road Kill concert. You said you needed some help getting ready for it."

"Well, why didn't you say so, sonny? Of course I do. You boys follow me. I'll show you what to do."

Amos fell in behind Dunc. "I hope this doesn't take too long. I really need to get those tickets this afternoon at the latest. They're selling out fast."

Mr. Whitman leaned close to Dunc. "Who's the skinny one with the beady eyes?"

11

"That's my friend, Mr. Whitman. He's going to help clean the center."

The little man looked Amos up and down, then he leaned close to Dunc again. "If I were you, son, I'd keep an eye on him."

Mr. Whitman unlocked the back door and hobbled down the stairs. He showed them where the cleaning supplies were kept. They were in a closet next to a door marked "Office."

"Is that your office, Mr. Whitman?" Dunc asked.

"No, sonny. The city doesn't see fit to give me an office. That's for those slick guys who manage the different shows that come in here. They use it while they're here, and then I clean it for the next show."

Mr. Whitman handed Dunc a mop and Amos a push broom. "You boys start up there in the balcony section and work your way down. It'll only take you two or three days to do the whole building." The little man slapped Amos on the back as he hobbled away. "Don't just stand there. Get to it, boy."

Amos tried to pick out the last row of seats in the shadows of the balcony. "Two or three days? This is going to take the rest of our lives."

"I wouldn't worry too much about it," a honey-smooth voice answered. A nice-looking young man, about twenty years old, walked up behind them. "The kids who come to the Road Kill concerts usually trash the place. If I were you, I wouldn't spend too much time cleaning up before the concert. It's after it that I'd worry about."

The young man stuck out his hand. "I'm Roy. Roy Freeman. I'm with the band."

Amos stared at him wide-eyed. "You're—you're Raunchy Roy." Amos was in shock.

The young man was embarrassed. "That's my stage name. My manager thought of it. You guys can call me Roy."

Amos continued to stand there with his mouth open. Dunc reached out and shook the young man's hand. "I'm Dunc." He jerked his thumb toward Amos. "This is Amos. He wanted to see your concert, so

13

we're cleaning the center to earn money to buy tickets."

"Hey, maybe I can help." Roy reached into his pocket and pulled out two tickets. "Here you go. On the house."

"Wow." Amos kept staring at him. "I actually know Raunchy Roy. Melissa is going to be so impressed."

"Who's Melissa?" Roy asked.

"This girl he's got a case for." Dunc headed for the supply closet. "It was nice meeting you, Roy. Come on, Amos. We better get busy, or we won't be through in time for the concert."

"Here." Roy reached into his pocket again. "If Amos is taking Melissa, you'll need another ticket."

Amos held up his hand. "Don't bother. Dunc thinks your music stinks."

Dunc gave Amos a hard look. "I didn't say it stinks."

"No, you're right. I think what you said was, they had the musical ability of leftover vegetables."

"Amos."

Roy smiled. "That's okay. I understand. Probably more than you know. Hey, I have an idea. How would you guys like to come to one of our practice sets? Who knows, maybe you'll hear something you'll like."

"Oh, hey, thanks for asking but—"

Amos stepped around Dunc. "Sounds great. We'll be there."

Chapter·3

They were in Dunc's kitchen making lunch. Amos bit into his newest creation—a sour pickle, whipped cream, and potato chip sandwich. His face puckered. "I think it needs something." Amos took another bite. "I don't want to rub it in or anything, but you were way off base about Raunchy Roy and the band."

Dunc put a piece of cheese on his ham sandwich. He carefully lined up the two slices of bread and cut off the crusts. "Maybe I *was* wrong about Roy. He seems like a nice enough guy when he isn't

17

dressed like an imitation Dracula and wearing that porcupine wig. But I wasn't wrong about his music. It's junk."

"You sound like my dad. Amy wanted to hear what Road Kill sounded like, so she took some of my hard-earned money and bought a CD. After my dad told her to turn it down for the third time, he completely lost it."

"What happened?"

"Let's just say, Amy's CD player is now a permanent fixture on our neighbor's roof."

"Oh."

"Don't waste pity on her. My mom felt bad about it, so she bought her tickets to see the concert. Can you believe it? Amy spends my money in the first place and ends up with free tickets too."

"Some people have all the luck."

"I'll say."

Dunc finished his sandwich. "Are you going down to listen to the band practice?"

"Yeah. Aren't you coming?"

"No. I think I'll stay home and work on my mold experiment."

18

"Great. I'll tell Roy and the band that you couldn't come because you had a pressing engagement with some mold."

"Maybe I'll come down later."

Amos grabbed another pickle. "It probably won't matter. I think they're getting used to things not working out for them. I was talking to Roy while you were disinfecting the handrails, and lately they've been having a string of bad luck that seems to follow them everywhere they go."

"Really?" Dunc sat up. "Like what?"

"Crazy stuff has been happening. One of the band members got locked in the bus right before they were supposed to go onstage in Texas. Two weeks ago, some of their equipment mysteriously disappeared right before a show. And last week, the electricity went out in the middle of a concert, and they had to refund all the tickets."

Dunc rubbed his chin. "Hmmm."

"Oh, no. Did you have to do that?"

"What?"

"Don't play innocent with me. I know what that sound means. *Trouble.* You al-

19

ways make that noise right before you convince me that we should stick our noses into somebody else's business."

Dunc took a bite of his sandwich. "This case has possibilities."

" 'This case'? I take it that means you're coming to the practice?"

"Wouldn't miss it."

Chapter · 4

Dunc opened the back door of the civic center with the key Mr. Whitman had given him earlier. "That's funny. I don't hear anything." He looked at his watch. "Roy said they'd be here at six, didn't he?"

Amos followed him down the balcony steps. "Maybe they decided to call off the practice."

The boys emerged through a dark passageway on the bottom floor, directly in front of the stage. The band's instruments were set up, but no one was there.

Amos started up the stage steps. Dunc

grabbed his sleeve. "Where do you think you're going?"

"Are you kidding? This is the opportunity of a lifetime. Haven't you ever wondered what it would be like to be up there playing to a huge audience?"

"I really don't think we should—"

It was too late. Amos was already sliding across the stage playing air guitar and pretending to sing to his fans.

Dunc started after him. "Amos, I'm serious. I think you better call it quits before you break something."

"What do you kids think you're doing?" a loud voice boomed at them from across the room.

The boys turned. A large man with a long red handlebar moustache was glaring at them from behind the opened door marked "Office."

The man stepped around the door and headed straight for them. Amos moved behind Dunc. "This area is off limits. How did you two get in here?"

Dunc cleared his throat. "Uhum. . . . We have a key. We're the cleaning crew."

"The cleaning crew. That's a good one! You little twirps are after an autograph, just like the rest of the dolts who listen to Road Kill."

Amos peeped out from behind Dunc. "That's not true, mister. It's like this. My friend here was trying to help me earn money because I flooded my mom's room and my sister stole my money, and Melissa likes these guys, so—"

"I'll give you punks exactly five seconds to clear out of here."

"Hold off, Mange." Roy and the band walked in from the stage door. "I invited them."

The redheaded man glared at him. "Are you out of your mind? You of all people should know we can't afford to trust anybody. You know what's been happening lately."

"These two are okay." Roy picked up his guitar. "They can stay."

Mange's look turned ugly. His eyes narrowed. He spun around and stomped back toward the office door.

"Whew." Amos sat on the stage steps. "That guy is scary."

"Don't let him bother you." Roy winked at them. "He thinks because he's our manager, and because he used to have his own band, that he's in charge around here."

The drummer, a thin guy with a long pointed nose, greasy hair, and beady eyes, sat down on his stool and picked up his sticks. "We gonna play or what?"

Roy frowned. "This charming fellow is Lizard. He's a heck of a drummer but a little short on manners. The one that looks like a mountain plays bass. We call him Horse. The lead guitar is Hairball."

The expressions on the band members' faces didn't change. They stared at the boys like stones.

Amos glanced from Horse to the one they called Hairball. He looked like a round puff of fuzz. It was hard to tell if there was even a body under all that hair unless he moved.

Dunc pulled Amos toward the first row of seats. "Why don't we just sit over here, out of your way, so you can practice?"

Roy laughed. "Don't mind these guys. They've been on the road so long, they've forgotten how to be normal."

The drummer hit his sticks together four times and the band started playing. They were loud and the song they were working on was about either smashing things and hurting people or running over a cow with a locomotive—Dunc couldn't quite tell which for sure.

When they were finished, Roy turned to the boys. "Well? What did you think?"

Dunc scratched his head. "To tell you the truth, Roy, I think it was—"

Amos elbowed him. "Interesting. He was about to say your music was definitely interesting."

After a few more songs, Roy turned to the band. "That's enough for today. You guys can go get some sleep. We'll practice again tomorrow before showtime." He sat down on the edge of the stage and hung his legs over the side. He looked at Dunc, who had a look on his face like he had just swallowed cod liver oil. "I can't say I blame you for not liking it. I'm not too crazy about it myself."

"Then why do you play it?" Dunc asked.

Roy shrugged. "Mange wrote it. He says it's the kind of music the kids want nowadays. Mange says if you want to stay on top, you have to play what kids like."

"Amos and I are kids, and we don't like it."

"Yes, we do," Amos blurted. "Well . . . sort of."

Roy looked up. "Maybe you have a point. If I had my way, I'd play my own stuff." He reached back for his guitar. "Songs like this one."

Roy started playing. The song had a rowdy beat, but the words were different from before. There were more of them—it actually had lyrics. It was a song about growing up in Roy's hometown. Amos started playing air guitar again. He was really getting into it. He moved up on the stage and twirled around. He accidentally tripped over Roy's guitar cord, pulling it out of the amp.

The music stopped short. Roy spun around to see what had happened just as a huge spotlight came hurtling down from the ceiling at him. Turning to look at Amos moved him sideways just enough to escape being hit as the spotlight smashed into the stage.

Chapter · 5

"Are you all right?" Dunc helped Roy to his feet.

"I think so." Roy brushed pieces of glass out of his hair. "That was too close for comfort."

"Sorry about unplugging your guitar cord," Amos said. "I guess I got a little carried away."

Roy looked at the heavy spotlight that was now lodged halfway through the stage floor. "I'm not sorry, Amos. If it hadn't been for you, I'd be dead meat right now."

Amos strained, trying to lift the spotlight. "I wonder what caused it to fall?"

Dunc examined the part that was sticking up. "Look at this. The bolts are gone, and the wires have all been cut. This was no accident, someone intended for it to fall."

Roy scratched his head. "Why would anybody want to do a thing like that?"

Dunc whipped a small note pad out of his shirt pocket and flipped it open. "Amos tells me you've been having a lot of unusual things happen to you lately."

"That's true, but nothing like this. Unless you count the time in Los Angeles when the backdrop came loose and fell forward over the top of us."

Dunc was writing furiously. "When did you first notice these strange occurrences?"

Roy rested his chin in his hand. "The first one was about a month ago, right before a concert. When our lead guitar player, Hairball, turned on his amp, we heard people talking on CB's. Someone had rewired his amplifier to pick up radio waves. We had to delay the concert."

30

Dunc looked up. "Do you always travel with the same band?"

Roy nodded. "Yup. These guys have been with me from the start. So has our manager, Mange. He's the one who put us together and came up with the name."

"Hmmm."

Amos sat down beside Roy and sighed. "There he goes with that noise again."

Roy raised one eyebrow. "Is that bad?"

"Depends on if you're his best friend or not. If you happen to have the misfortune of being his best friend, then it means he's about to get you in some serious trouble."

Roy looked confused.

Amos waved his hand. "Don't worry about it. Dunc thinks he's some kind of junior private eye. He goes around digging up imaginary cases to solve."

"This one doesn't sound so imaginary." Dunc closed his notebook. "Somebody wants to put a stop to Raunchy Roy and Road Kill. And today they almost put a stop to Roy— permanently."

Chapter · 6

"How should I word this?" Amos was at his desk trying to compose a letter to Melissa. His plan was to drop the letter and the ticket in her mailbox later that afternoon, ring the doorbell, and run away.

Dunc was sitting on the floor concentrating on a formula for solving the case. He had chosen the floor because right now it was the safest place in Amos's room. There were piles of stuff everywhere. Amos's mom had told him to get his room organized or else plan on living at the YMCA. So he de-

33

cided to put everything into piles according to size or possible use. He had a pile of paper wads for shooting at the trash, a pile of dirty socks, a pile of moldy food he was saving for Dunc's experiment, and several other piles that fell into the category of miscellaneous junk.

Dunc had to move the dirty jean pile next to the soda can pile before he could sit down. "Why don't you just tell Melissa that you have these tickets and ask her to go to the concert with you?"

Amos shook his head. "No style. I want this letter to really make an impression on her."

"What do you have so far?"

Amos smoothed the piece of paper and cleared his throat. " 'Dear Melissa. How do I love thee? Let me count the ways. I love thee to the—' "

"Hold it. I think that one's been done."

Amos scratched his head. "Are you sure?"

Dunc nodded. "Pretty sure."

"Okay then, I'll skip that part. How about this. 'At enormous personal expense I have obtained this priceless ticket—' "

Dunc stopped him again. "Amos, you didn't pay anything for that ticket. It was free."

"Details." Amos cleared his throat again. "Where was I? Oh yeah—'to this once-in-a-lifetime opportunity—' "

"Amos, it's not once in a lifetime. Road Kill is giving two concerts."

"I know that. Give me a break. I'm trying to be creative here."

"Is that what you call it?"

Amos scanned the letter. " 'For the experience of a lifetime, meet me at the civic center at six-thirty on Friday, and together we'll attend the social event of the year. I will be counting the seconds until we meet. Yours eternally. Signed, your adoring admirer.' " Amos looked up. "Well, what do you think?"

Dunc tried not to smile. "I don't know. It may be too low-key."

Amos studied the letter. "I didn't want to come on too strong. It might scare her off."

"Why didn't you sign your name? How is she supposed to know who sent her the ticket?"

"Mystery."

"I'm not following you."

"I checked out this real informative book from the library called *How to Attract Girls in One Easy Lesson*. It said girls go nuts over stuff like this. They think it's romantic. When I meet her in front of the civic center wearing my black tuxedo with tails and carrying an armful of red roses, she'll know who sent the letter. Then we'll get engaged and pick out a china pattern."

Dunc erased some figures on his note pad. "I didn't know you had a tuxedo. And where are you going to get the money for an armful of roses?"

"I'm not sure about the tux yet, but I've got the roses worked out. Mrs. McGillis down on First Street had a bumper crop of roses this year."

"Amos, you can't just go pick some poor old lady's roses."

"She gave me permission."

"For a whole armful?"

"Not exactly. But she did say if I mowed her back yard, I could have a few."

"I hope it works out for you." Dunc turned his attention back to his notes. "Boy, this case has me baffled. So far I can't figure out any reason for somebody to be sabotaging the Road Kill band. What we need is more clues."

"What we need is to let them solve their own problems. I know you. You're going to get us involved in some big deal and end up messing up my date with Melissa."

Dunc put his hand over his heart. "Amos, would I put a case before my best friend's happiness?"

"In a heartbeat."

"Okay, just to show you how wrong you are about me, I'll even go with you to put the letter in Melissa's mailbox."

"Why?"

"Like I said, you're my best friend—and besides, Melissa's house isn't too far from the civic center. We can stop by there before we come home and see if we can dig up some more clues."

Chapter·7

"Do you think Melissa's dad bought any of that?" Amos pedaled up beside Dunc.

"I think you had him right up until the part where you tried to convince him you were a dwarf working for the post office." Dunc stood on his pedals. "Too bad he had to come out of the house just as you were going through his mail."

"I wasn't going through his mail. I was trying to put Melissa's letter in the middle of the pile so it wouldn't be so obvious."

"It looked like you were going through his mail."

Amos parked his bike next to Dunc's in the rack behind the civic center. "At least he took my letter. Do you think he meant what he said about stuffing me into the mailbox if he ever saw me near their house again?"

"Probably."

Amos sighed. "Something like that could definitely put a strain on our future relationship as in-laws."

Dunc turned the key in the back door of the civic center and pushed it open. "Looks like everyone's gone."

Amos followed him through the door and down the steps to the stage. "That's because they all know how dumb it would be to spend your afternoon in a big empty building."

"You go backstage and see what you can find. I'll look around out here."

Amos climbed the stage steps and disappeared behind the curtain. In a few seconds he poked his head back through the curtain. "What am I looking for?"

"Something that might help us figure out what's been going on around here."

"Right." Amos pulled his head back and looked around. The backstage area was sectioned off with partitions. In one corner the lighting and special effects were set up. In another corner the band's costumes and face paint were set out, ready for Friday's performance.

"This is so dumb." Amos halfheartedly poked around in the lighting section. "What does he think we're going to find? A note with a signed confession?"

He moved to the makeup table. There were two half-gallon tubs of green and black face paint. "Boy, when these guys paint their faces, they get serious."

Amos dipped his finger in the green paint and held it up to his nose. "Yechh! How can they stand to wear this stuff? It smells worse than Dunc's lab experiments." He looked up at the mirror and noticed a tiny green spot where his finger had touched the end of his nose. He wiped at it but succeeded only in spreading it around a little. The harder he rubbed, the worse it got. In seconds his nose was completely bright green.

"Dunc!"

Dunc raced up the stairs and pulled the curtain back. "Did you find something?"

Amos turned around. He looked like he had a small watermelon stuck in the center of his face.

"What did you—"

"Never mind. Help me get it off."

"You need makeup remover." Dunc picked up some of the jars on the table. "I don't see any. They must keep it on the bus."

"A lot of good that does me. What am I supposed to do? Ride home like this?"

"We'll go the back way through the woods. Nobody will see you. When we get to my house, we'll use some of my mom's stuff to get it off."

Amos headed for the door.

"Wait." Dunc caught up with him. "I found something. It might be a clue."

"Who cares? I have to get home before someone sees me like this and it ruins my reputation."

"What reputation?"

"The one I'm never going to have if I go around with a zucchini nose."

"It'll only take a minute."

"Oh, all right. Where is it?"

"Right over here." Dunc led the way to the edge of the stage. From the corner, tucked behind a speaker, he pulled a small toolchest with the name *Mange Roper* written across the top.

Amos made a face. "You call this a clue? Get serious."

Dunc opened the box and took out a set of wrenches. "This is the clue."

"So? One of the wrenches is missing. Big deal."

"The one that's missing would have fit the bolts on the spotlight perfectly."

"So now you're Mister Fix-it, who knows everything about wrenches and stuff."

Amos turned and made for the balcony door. "Did it ever occur to you that even if you're right about the wrench, anybody could have taken it? It didn't have to be Mange."

Dunc stepped beside him. "I thought about that. But he's still our number-one suspect."

Amos unlocked his bike. "Why?"

"Because right now he's our only suspect."

Amos wasn't listening. A group of girls was coming toward them from the library. Amos dropped his bicycle.

The one in the middle was Melissa.

A couple of the girls giggled when they saw Amos's nose. Melissa didn't seem to notice him at all. She waved at Dunc and walked on down the sidewalk.

Chapter · 8

Amos was sitting on the end of Dunc's bed with an inch of cold cream on his nose. "I don't get it. Why do these things always happen to me?"

Dunc rubbed his chin. "I've been giving that some thought. I'd say it has something to do with the amount of space per person multiplied by the number of points of time in a given year, minus the refractory equation—of course taking into account the probability of happpenstance."

"What does all that boil down to in plain English?"

"Luck."

Amos sagged. "Melissa will probably want to cancel our date now. She'll be too embarrassed to be seen with me."

"How is she going to cancel it? She doesn't even know who it's with. You didn't sign your name to the letter, remember?"

Amos sat up. "That's true. And when she sees the roses and candy, she'll probably forget all about it."

"Candy?"

"In case she's allergic to the roses."

"Oh." Dunc turned on his computer and started entering information. "It doesn't make sense."

Amos lay back on the bed. "Sure it does. If Melissa starts sneezing, I can ditch the roses and bring out the candy. Either way, I'm covered."

"Not that. The case. Why would Mange want to put a stop to the Road Kill concerts? He probably makes a bundle of money off of each one. If they were to stop, he'd be out of a job."

Amos shrugged. "Maybe he has a personal problem with one of the guys in the band."

"That's a possibility. But would you give up all that money just because you have a problem with somebody?"

"Nope. Looks like you're fresh out of a suspect."

Dunc studied his computer screen. "Not necessarily. What we need is more evidence, something that will show us what Mange has to gain from all of this."

"If you're so sure it's him, why don't you go to the police? They'll go down to his office with a warrant and find the evidence they need to arrest him."

"That's it." Dunc snapped his fingers. "Why didn't I think of it before?"

"Dunc, I was kidding. Nobody in their right mind would—"

"The office. Amos, we need to get inside Mange's office. There's probably all kinds of incriminating stuff in there. We'll leave early tomorrow morning before anybody's awake."

Dunc leaned back in his chair and folded

his arms. "We'll have this case solved before lunch, and the Road Kill band can go on-stage tomorrow night as scheduled with nothing to worry about."

"I hate to burst your bubble, Sherlock, but I'm busy tomorrow morning."

Both front legs of Dunc's chair hit the floor. "What could possibly be more important than saving someone's career?"

"Saving my room from the Salvation Army. My mom didn't appreciate the way I organized the stuff, so she called the Salvation Army and told them to bring a truck. A *big* truck."

"Come on, Amos. You have to help me. We could be saving lives here."

"No way. My whole life is in that room. I'm not just going to stand by and let complete strangers come in and carry it off."

Amos had his mind made up, and Dunc knew there was no changing it, unless . . . "I understand perfectly, Amos. You go ahead and stay home tomorrow morning. I'll go down to the civic center by myself. It's okay."

Amos eyed him suspiciously. "Why are you giving up so fast? It's not like you."

Dunc turned off his computer. "I wouldn't want you to be gone during an important thing like a visit from the Salvation Army."

"What's the catch?"

"There's no catch. Of course, when the band calls me up onstage during the concert and personally thanks me in front of everybody, including Melissa, and I get all the glory for solving the case, you'll have to sit there and settle for knowing that you stayed home and did what you thought was more important."

"You think they'll call us up onstage?"

"I'm almost sure of it."

Amos chewed on a fingernail. "When you stop and think about it, I guess some of that stuff in my room could stand to be cleared away."

Dunc smiled. "Whatever you say, Amos."

Chapter · 9

Dunc tripped over the pile of broken models and used tubes of glue at the foot of Amos's bed. He stopped and listened.

Nothing.

Everybody was still asleep. He leaned down close to Amos's ear. "Wake up. We've got major undercover work to do, remember?"

Amos opened one eye. "Go away. I'm doing my own undercover work right here." He jerked the covers up over his head and turned over.

Dunc frowned. He considered calling

Scruff, the Binders' border collie. Scruff hated Amos and would be more than happy to be a part of anything that would irritate him. Dunc had successfully used him in the past to get Amos out of bed, but he knew if he whistled, he might wake someone else. He decided not to risk it. Instead he looked around the room and moved to one of the piles.

The dirty sock pile.

Dunc held his own nose and quietly swung a stiff, smelly sock back and forth under Amos's nose. The cold cream had worked. Amos's nose was pink again, but now it wrinkled and turned white; then his lip curled. He sputtered and gagged, then sat bolt upright.

"Ugggh!" Amos knocked the sock out of his hand. "That's not fair. You used chemical warfare."

"Shhh." Dunc put his finger to his lips. "You want to wake up the whole house?"

"If I have to get up, they can too."

"If your parents get up, they might want

you to explain where you're going at this time of the morning."

"So? I'll explain."

"They might not let you go."

Amos fell back on his pillow. "Then that's all the more reason to wake them up."

Dunc took Amos by the legs and swung him around sideways. Then he grabbed him by the arms and pulled until he had him in a sitting position. "Come on, Amos. This is important."

"You always say that. It never turns out that way, but it doesn't stop you from saying it."

Dunc ignored him. "Where are your clothes?"

Amos pointed to a pile near the middle of the room. "Take the ones on top."

"You're going to wear clothes from a pile on the floor?"

Amos nodded. "Saves time. No folding and unfolding. No hangers to worry about. After I'm through with them, I put them in that pile over there." He pointed to a stack of dirty clothes. "It's a great system. I thought of it myself. I'm thinking of having it patented. I'll probably make a ton of money."

"Too bad your mother's not as crazy about it as you are."

Amos yawned. "I know. Some people just don't know a good thing when they see it. If this were to catch on, I'd be rich. Then my dad could retire, and I could hire a maid, install a swimming pool, pay someone to take my sister away—"

Dunc handed him his clothes. "Get dressed. We don't have a lot of time."

Chapter · 10

Amos let the big metal door slam shut behind him.

"Shhh!" Dunc glared at him. "We don't want anybody to know we're in here."

"I thought you said no one would be up at this hour."

"First rule of surveillance—you can never be too careful."

"Where did you learn that? The Handy Home School of Spying?"

"Cute. Stay behind me, and try to be quiet."

Dunc inched his way along the wall

toward the office. Amos followed, even though he was sure the whole thing was a waste of time.

"Wait." Dunc held up his hand. "I'll see if the coast is clear."

Amos rolled his eyes. "Whatever."

Dunc moved to the door. He motioned for Amos to come closer.

"Are we through playing secret agent yet?"

Dunc clapped his hand over Amos's mouth. A voice was coming from inside the office. Someone was talking on the phone.

"Yes, is this the Grenfield Insurance Agency?"

The boys sat on their heels and waited.

"Hello, Mr. Grenfield. This is Mange Roper. Listen, I was just calling to double-check the terms on that policy I have with you on the Road Kill band. . . . I wanted to make sure that if the concert is canceled for any reason, I'll still be able to collect the insurance money. . . ."

Dunc's eyes widened. He pointed to the

balcony. The boys tiptoed away from the office and then blasted up the balcony steps and out the door.

Amos stopped to catch his breath, but Dunc kept going. "Hey, wait for me."

Dunc didn't slow down. He jumped on his bike and took off. He was already in his room making plans when Amos staggered in.

"Where's the fire?" Amos plopped on Dunc's bed. "The way you're acting, you'd think it was a matter of life and death."

"It might be, Amos. Didn't you hear Mange on the phone? He collects insurance money every time the band can't go on. There's probably no telling what he might do to keep them from appearing tonight."

"So go tell Roy. He'll call the police, and they'll put Mange away. Simple."

"I can't just go tell Roy a thing like this. He's known Mange a long time. He'll want proof."

"If he waits for much more proof, he may wind up in the hospital."

"There's only one thing to do." Dunc stood up. "We have to keep an eye on the band until after the concert."

"You mean *you* have to keep an eye on them. I have a date, remember?"

"But Amos—"

Amos held up his hand. "It won't work. Nothing you can say will convince me. Thanks to you, my bedroom is being ransacked by total strangers. I've done my duty for the day. I'm not giving up a date with Melissa for anything."

"Not even if they call you up onstage?"

Amos shook his head. "Not even for that."

"Maybe we don't have to watch them all day. Maybe we can stop Mange if we just go down there a little early and hang around. He won't try anything with witnesses."

"How early is early?"

"Not too early."

"Dunc."

"A few hours. You can take your flowers and tux with you. It'll be fine. You wanted to get there before Melissa. What's a few hours? This way at least you'll be on time."

"I'd have to get ready for my date in a public bathroom."

"I'll stick an 'out of order' sign on the door. It'll be fine. Trust me."

"You had to say that. 'Trust me.' You had to say that, didn't you?"

Chapter · 11

"How do I look?" Amos stepped out of the civic center bathroom carrying an armful of flowers and a large box of candy.

Dunc walked around him. "Where did you get the tuxedo?"

"Ace's Rent-A-Tux. It took almost everything I made from cleaning this place. Why? Is something wrong?"

"It looks like it would fit your dad. The tails almost drag on the ground."

"Ace told me they were having a big dance at the college, and this was the best he could do on short notice. He even helped me roll up the sleeves. Do you think anyone will notice?"

Dunc crossed his fingers behind his back and shook his head. "No. You look fine."

"What about these?" Amos held out the flowers he had picked from Mrs. McGillis's garden. "Aren't they great?"

"Real nice. But next time, you might try cutting them instead of pulling them up by the roots."

"So that's how they do it! Oh well, if she doesn't go for them, there's always the candy." Amos took the box from under his arm.

"Gee, Amos. Now I'm impressed. Those chocolates must have set you back a few bucks."

"Not really." Amos took off the lid. "I borrowed the empty box from my mom's closet and filled the holes with jelly beans from our candy dish downstairs. Want some?"

"I'll pass. We better get back out front if we're going to keep an eye on Mange. So far he hasn't been able to make a move."

"Do you think he knows we're watching him?"

"I can't tell. But it doesn't matter as long as it keeps him from trying anything."

It was still forty-five minutes until showtime. The lighting and sound crew were making last-minute adjustments onstage. So far, nothing unusual had happened. Mange had come out of his office twice to check on things. Each time, he gave some orders and then went back in the office and slammed the door.

The office door opened again. Mange stomped past the stage and headed for the exit.

"Now's our chance." Dunc motioned for Amos to follow him.

"Our chance for what?"

"To get those insurance papers. If we can show them to Roy, he'll have to believe us. You guard the door while I look for them. If Mange comes back, signal me."

Amos grabbed his flowers and candy and positioned himself in front of the door. "Hey, Dunc."

"What? Is he coming?"

"No. I just wondered if you knew what to do for wilting flowers? These are starting to look pretty sad."

"Throw them away and give her the candy."

"I can't. You made me miss my dinner and I was starving. I just ate all the candy."

Dunc was searching through Mange's briefcase. He found an envelope with the name *Grenfield* on it. "I think this is it. Keep watching while I make sure."

Amos was trying to prop up his sagging roses. He stuck them under the drinking fountain and turned it on. It didn't help, and now he had wet, sagging roses. He was about to shake the water off when he looked up. Mange had come back and was standing in front of the stage talking to one of the hands. Amos ducked inside the office and pulled the door shut behind him. "Quick, hide. Mange is right outside."

Dunc stuffed the policy in his shirt and searched for a place to hide. There wasn't any. The office was too small.

The boys looked at each other in panic. They could hear Mange's heavy footsteps coming toward them. He was talking to someone. "Give me a minute, Fred. I forgot to lock the office."

Dunc held his breath. He watched the doorknob turn. Then he heard a click and the sound of footsteps walking away.

"Whew!" Amos wiped the perspiration off his forehead. "That was a close one."

Dunc slumped down in the armchair. "Don't look now. But I think we're locked in."

"What? We can't be locked in. I have a date with Melissa in"—Amos looked at his watch—"exactly thirteen minutes." He tried the door. It wouldn't budge. His shoulders drooped. "I knew it," he said. "It never fails. Every time I go along with one of your stupid plans, something goes wrong."

Dunc was studying the ceiling.

"Are you listening to me? The girl of my dreams is out there, and I can't get to her. My life is ruined."

Dunc stood on the chair. He pulled on the air-conditioner vent. It came loose in his hands.

"I hope you don't think I'm going to climb up there." Amos backed away from him. "You can just include me out. This is a rented outfit."

"Suit yourself." Dunc jumped and grabbed the edge where the vent used to be. He pulled himself up and in. He turned and looked down. "Plenty of room in here for two."

Amos sat in the chair. He looked at his flowers, thought about Melissa, and sighed. "She'll wait outside for a while and then realize she's been stood up. It'll break her heart. She'll probably go straight home and cry her eyes out. It'll scar her for life." He stood on the chair and pulled himself up into the shaft.

"I thought you weren't coming." Dunc was already a few feet down the shaft.

Amos scrambled over the top of him. "Do you think I'd let Melissa wind up a total wreck over this?"

"Wait up, Amos. How do you know which direction to take?"

"I can hear talking. They must be letting people in now. We'll head in this direction until we find another vent, drop out, and find Melissa."

They crawled in the dark passage for what seemed to Amos like years.

"Maybe we should have turned left at that last side shaft," Dunc said.

Amos sat down. "It's no use. We'll never get out of here in time for the concert."

"Wait." Dunc started moving. "I hear music."

"That's just great. They've already started without us."

"Come on, Amos. We'll move toward the music. The louder it gets, the closer we are to the auditorium. There are bound to be vents there somewhere."

They crawled until the music was so loud, they could hardly hear each other talk.

Dunc stopped and yelled, "I found a vent, but I can't get the cover off."

Amos helped, but they couldn't budge it. Dunc studied the situation. He knew this might be their last chance.

"Wait, Amos. Is that Melissa I see down there?"

Amos pressed his face to the vent. "Where? I don't see anything."

"Right there. In the front row with Biff Fastrack."

That's all it took. Amos dived at the vent. His face crashed through it, and he found himself looking down at the stage. He would have landed on his head right in the center of the stage, except his luck cut in and the tails of his tuxedo caught the sharp edge of the air-conditioner shaft. He hung there, suspended in midair, swinging back and forth like a chandelier in front of a packed house.

Chapter · 12

"Thanks for getting me down. I was starting to get dizzy up there."

"No problem." Roy grinned. "Luckily the song we were playing was called 'Don't Keep Me Hanging.' The audience thought you were part of the show. I'm just sorry you had to wait until intermission so we could close the curtain. What were you two doing up there, anyway?"

Dunc pulled the insurance papers out of his shirt. "We know who's behind all the mysterious things that have been happening to your band."

"You do?"

Dunc nodded and held out Mange's policy. "Take a look at this. Mange gets a pile of insurance money each time you guys don't play."

Roy stared at the policy in Dunc's hand without taking it.

"Do you want us to call the cops?" Amos asked.

Roy sighed. "No. I guess it's time to come clean. Mange isn't the one behind all the problems—I am."

"You?!" Dunc dropped the papers, and Amos did a double-take. "I don't understand," Dunc said.

Roy sat down on the stage floor. "It's a long story. I never meant to hurt anybody. Even that stunt with the spotlight was rigged. I knew it was going to fall all the time. I made sure I was the only one standing in that spot when it did, and I stepped aside."

"I still don't get it."

"I just wanted out. All of this"—Roy waved his arm—"it's not for me. I don't like having a green face and weird hair. And I especially don't like doing songs that talk about hurting people and tearing things up."

"Wouldn't it have been easier just to quit?" Amos asked.

"I *couldn't* quit. My contract is good for three more years. I thought if I caused enough things to go wrong, the other guys would call it off. Then there wouldn't be a band. Without a band, I'd be free to start over again."

Dunc tapped his chin. "Hmmm. This gives me an idea."

"Not again," Amos moaned.

"There just might be an easy way around all of this."

Chapter · 13

Dunc put the letter in his pocket and rang the doorbell. Mrs. Binder let him in. He raced past her and took the stairs two at a time. The door to Amos's room was open. Dunc started to go in. He stopped. For a minute he thought he was in the wrong room.

It was clean.

For the first time Dunc could remember, Amos's room was entirely clean. There was nothing on the floor, and you could actually see the bed.

"Wow!"

"Don't rub it in." Amos was sitting on the floor in a corner eating a banana. "This is all your fault, you know. The Salvation Army cleaned me out. I'm lucky they left the bed."

"This is great, Amos. I never knew you had carpet in here."

"Very funny."

Dunc pulled the letter out of his pocket. "It's from Roy."

"How does he like his new singing career as just plain old Roy Freeman?"

Dunc skimmed the letter. "He says he's doing great, and Road Kill is also doing fine with its new leader. Mange is really packing them in."

Amos threw the banana peel at the trash can and missed. "That was a great idea you had about replacing Raunchy Roy with Menacing Mange. I guess Mange never really wanted to be a manager. He was always a musician at heart. But even I was surprised when he let Roy out of his contract."

"Looks like everything's working out.

Roy sent you a ticket to his first concert. He says he knows you probably can't make it to Cincinnati, but he feels bad about your date with Melissa and everything."

"Actually that worked out okay too. It turned out that Melissa never wanted to go to the concert. She likes classical music. I heard she threw the ticket in the trash."

"That's too bad, considering all the trouble you went through."

Amos shrugged. "It's okay. Hey, I wonder if she'd be interested in going to a Roy Freeman concert."

"In Cincinnati?"

"Yeah, I could rent another tux, get some plastic flowers so they won't wilt on me. This time maybe I'll hire a limo. What do you think?"

Dunc sighed. "It's going to be an interesting year."

Be sure to join Dunc and Amos in these other Culpepper Adventures:

The Case of the Dirty Bird

When Dunc Culpepper and his best friend, Amos, first see the parrot in a pet store, they're not impressed—it's smelly, scruffy, and missing half its feathers. They're only slightly impressed when they learn that the parrot speaks four languages, has outlived ten of its owners, and is probably 150 years old. But when the bird starts mouthing off about buried treasure, Dunc and Amos get pretty excited—let the amateur sleuthing begin!

Dunc's Doll

Dunc and his accident-prone friend Amos are up to their old sleuthing habits once again. This time they're after a band of doll thieves! When a doll that once belonged to Charles Dickens's daughter is stolen from an exhibition at the local mall, the two boys put on their detective gear and do some serious snooping. Will a vicious watchdog keep them from retrieving the valuable missing doll?

Culpepper's Cannon

Dunc and Amos are researching the Civil War cannon that stands in the town square when they find a note inside telling them about a time portal. Entering it through the dressing room of La Petite, a women's clothing store, the boys find themselves in downtown Chatham on March 8, 1862—the day before the historic clash between the *Monitor* and the *Merrimac*. But the Confederate soldiers they meet mistake them for Yankee spies. Will they make it back to the future in one piece?

Dunc Gets Tweaked

Dunc and Amos meet up with a new buddy named Lash when they enter the radical world of skateboard competition. When somebody "cops"—steals—Lash's prototype skateboard, the boys are determined to get it back. After all, Lash is about to shoot for a totally rad world's record! Along the way they learn a major lesson: *Never* kiss a monkey!

Dunc's Halloween

Dunc and Amos are planning the best route to get the most candy on Halloween. But their plans change when Amos is slightly bitten by a werewolf. He begins scratching himself and chasing UPS trucks—he's become a werepuppy!

Dunc Breaks the Record

Dunc and Amos have a small problem when they try hang gliding—they crash in the wilderness. Luckily, Amos has read a book about a boy who survived in the wilderness for fifty-four days. Too bad Amos doesn't have a hatchet. Things go from bad to worse when a wild man holds the boys captive. Can anything save them now?

Dunc and the Flaming Ghost

Dunc's not afraid of ghosts, although Amos is sure that the old Rambridge house is haunted by the ghost of Blackbeard the Pirate. Then the best friends meet Eddie, a meek man who claims to be impersonating Blackbeard's ghost in order to live in the house in peace. But if that's true, why are flames shooting from his mouth?

Amos Gets Famous

Deciphering a code they find in a library book, Amos and Dunc stumble onto a burglary ring. The burglars' next target is the home of Melissa, the girl of Amos's dreams (who doesn't even know that he's alive). Amos longs to be a hero to Melissa, so nothing will stop him from solving this case—not even a mind-boggling collision with a jock, a chimpanzee, and a toilet.

Dunc and Amos Hit the Big Top

In order to impress Melissa, Amos decides to perform on the trapeze at the visiting circus. Look out below! But before Dunc can talk him out of his plan, the two stumble across a mystery behind the scenes at the circus. Now Amos is in double trouble. What's really going on under the big top?

Dunc's Dump

Camouflaged as piles of rotting trash, Dunc and Amos are sneaking around the town dump. Dunc wants to find out who is polluting the garbage at the dump with hazardous and toxic waste. Amos just wants to impress Melissa. Can either of them succeed?

Dunc and the Scam Artists

Dunc and Amos are at it again. Some older residents of their town have been bilked by con artists, and the two boys want to look into these crimes. They meet elderly Betsy Dell, whose nasty nephew Frank gives the boys the creeps. Then they notice some soft dirt in Ms. Dell's shed, and a shovel. Does Frank have something horrible in store for Dunc and Amos?

Dunc and Amos and the Red Tattoos

Dunc and Amos head for camp and face two weeks of fresh air—along with regulations, demerits, KP, and inedible food. But where these two best friends go, trouble follows. They overhear a threat against the camp director and discover that camp funds have been stolen. Do these crimes have anything to do with the tattoo of the exotic red flower that some of the camp staff have on their arms?

Dunc's Undercover Christmas

It's Christmastime! and Dunc, Amos, and Amos's cousin T.J. hit the mall for some serious shopping. But when the seasonal magic is threatened by some disappearing presents, and

Santa Claus himself is a prime suspect, the boys put their celebration on hold and go undercover in perfect Christmas disguises! Can the sleuthing trio protect Santa's threatened reputation and catch the impostor before he strikes again?

The Wild Culpepper Cruise

When Amos wins a "Why I Love My Dog" contest, he and Dunc are off on the Caribbean cruise of their dreams! But there's something downright fishy about Amos's suitcase, and before they know it, the two best friends wind up with more high-seas adventure than they bargained for. Can Dunc and Amos figure out who's out to get them and salvage what's left of their vacation?

Dunc and the Haunted Castle

When Dunc and Amos are invited to spend a week in Scotland, Dunc can already hear the bagpipes a-blowin'. But when the boys spend their first night in an ancient castle, it isn't bagpipes they hear. It's moans! Dunc hears groaning coming from inside his bedroom walls. Amos notices that the eyes of a painting follow him across the room! Could the castle really be haunted? Local legend has it that the castle's former lord wanders the ramparts at night in search of his head! Team up with Dunc and Amos as they go ghostbusting in the Scottish Highlands!

Cowpokes and Desperadoes

Git along, little dogies! Dunc and Amos are bound for Uncle Woody Culpepper's Santa Fe cattle ranch for a week of fun. But when they overhear a couple of cowpokes plotting to do Uncle Woody in, the two sleuths are back on the trail of some serious action! Who's been making off with all the prize cattle? Can Dunc and Amos stop the rustlers in time to save the ranch?

Prince Amos

When their fifth-grade class spends a weekend interning at the state capitol, Dunc and Amos find themselves face-to-face with Amos's walking double—Prince Gustav, Crown Prince of Moldavia! His Royal Highness is desperate to uncover a traitor in his ranks. And when he asks Amos to switch places with him, Dunc holds his breath to see what will happen next. Can Amos pull off the impersonation of a lifetime?

Coach Amos

Amos and Dunc have their hands full when their school principal asks *them* to coach a local T-ball team. For one thing, nobody on the team even knows first base from left field, and the season opener is coming right up. And then there's that sinister-looking gangster driving by in his long black limo and making threats. Can Dunc and Amos fend off screaming tots, nervous mothers, and the mob, and be there when the ump yells, "Play ball"?

Amos and the Alien

When Amos and his best friend, Dunc, have a close encounter with an extraterrestrial named Girrk, Dunc thinks they should report their findings to NASA. But Amos has other plans. He not only promises to help Girrk find a way back to his planet, he invites him to hide out under his bed! Then weird things start to happen—Scruff can't move, Amos scores a game-winning *touchdown,* and Dunc knows Girrk is behind Amos's new powers. What's the mysterious alien really up to?

Dunc and Amos Meet the Slasher

Why is mild-mannered Amos dressed in leather, with slicked-back hair, strutting around the cafeteria and going by a phony name? Could it be because of that new kid, Slasher, who's promised to eat Amos for his lunch? Or has Amos secretly gone undercover? Amos and his pal Dunc have some hot leads and are close to cracking a stolen stereo racket, but Dunc is worried Amos has taken things too far!

Dunc and the Greased Sticks of Doom

Five . . . four . . . three . . . two . . . Olympic superstar Francesco Bartoli is about to hurl himself down the face of a mountain in another attempt to clinch the world slalom speed record. Cheering fans and snapping cameras are everywhere. But someone is out to stop him, and Dunc thinks he knows who it is. Can Dunc get to the gate in time to save the day? Will Amos survive longer than fifteen minutes on the icy slopes?

DATE DUE

MAR 2 9 1999			
MAR 0 2 2001			
	DISCARD		
GAYLORD			PRINTED IN U.S.A